Musings

75 Short Stories

Don Tassone

Gordon,

Thanks for all your
support.

Best,

Don

Copyright © 2023 Don Tassone

Toerner Press

3395 St. George's Way

Loveland, Ohio 45140

Print ISBN: 979-8-218-13802-8

Cover design by Maggie Toerner

Contents

Mystery

Discovery

Fantasy

Light

Shadow

Nostalgia

Fun

For Liz

Acknowledgements

I want to thank my wife Liz, Libby Belle, Kathy Kennedy and Patti Normile for their help and encouragement on these stories and Maggie Toerner for designing the cover of this book.

I also want to extend grateful acknowledgment to the editors of the online literary magazines where the original versions of many of these stories appeared: *Friday Flash Fiction, Literary Yard, Terror House Magazine* and *The Birdseed*.

Don Tassone

Preface

Ideas for most of my stories come from real-life events. When I reflect on these events, themes emerge. Ordinary occurrences take on deeper meaning.

The 75 new stories in this collection come from my own musings about happenings in the world and in my life.

I hope these little stories show what pausing to reflect can reveal. I hope they might also invite a closer look at the passing parade of events through our daily lives.

Don Tassone

Mystery

The Encounter

From the side, the man in front of me in the grocery checkout line looked like my childhood friend Rick, whom I hadn't seen for decades. But I figured he was too old.

He seemed to sense my stare and looked back at me. I had just come from the office and was wearing a business suit, quite a contrast with the man's shabby clothes. His long, tangled hair made me feel like I'd just come from the barber.

He opened his mouth a little, as if to speak. But then he turned away.

I wondered what he was going to say. Maybe it was Rick after all.

We'd grown up on the same street. We walked to grade school together. Everyone liked Rick. He was smart, good-hearted and funny.

He had big dreams too. When we were kids, Rick wanted to be an astronaut. When we were teenagers, he told us he was going to be President one day. No one doubted him. Our senior year in high school, Rick was our class president. We voted him most likely to succeed.

But just after we graduated, Rick's mother died unexpectedly. I went to the funeral. Rick was inconsolable.

That summer, I stopped by Rick's house, but he wouldn't see me. Other friends tried to reach out too, but Rick wouldn't engage. He seemed to change overnight. I wasn't altogether surprised when Rick didn't go off to college that fall.

But I wasn't expecting him to disappear. I hadn't seen Rick in 40 years, but I thought of him often and hoped he was okay.

Maybe it was simply wishful thinking, but this guy in front of me sure looked like an old, ragged version of my old friend.

"Rick?" I said.

His body stiffened, but he didn't turn around.

"Rick, is that you?"

He didn't answer. Instead, he put his groceries on the belt. Not wanting to be a pest, I didn't say anything more.

A few minutes later, the cashier handed the man his receipt. He began to push his cart away but stopped and looked back at me.

"Bob," he said with a nod and a small, knowing smile.

Then he pushed on and left.

Where is Everybody?

I had learned not to try to go into restaurants because they were no longer open for dining. Another casualty of Covid, I thought.

But I was shocked when the drive-thru of my favorite burger joint was closed "due to staff shortage."

So I decided to stop at the grocery store to pick up food for dinner. But a sign on the door said, "Closed. We're sorry. Staff shortage. Try our autonomous vehicle delivery."

Hospitals are closing units. Not enough nurses.

Airlines are cutting routes. Not enough pilots.

Pools aren't opening this summer. Not enough lifeguards.

Where is everybody?

The Leaf

He runs every day on a trail along a river under a canopy of trees.

He watches a yellow leaf float down and land in the still-green grass. Five months ago these trees were budding out. He is mindful that, to the leaf, five months is a lifetime.

He wonders if the leaf and the tree miss one another. He thinks about the leaf disintegrating, dissolving into the Earth, becoming one with another tree.

The season is changing. His pace is slowing. His stride is growing shorter. He wonders if one day, like the leaf, he will begin anew.

Post-Holiday Wish

Try as he might, David couldn't escape the noise and commotion. All he wanted was some peace.

He knew, of course, it came with the holidays. The constant stream of parties and guests, too much indulging and too little sleep, having his daily routine torn apart like wrapping paper. This year, though, it had really worn him down.

Then, at last, the holidays were over. David slept in and made himself some coffee. He sat sipping it in silence. It was the quiet morning he had longed for, yet he found the sudden stillness unsettling.

I hope someone drops by today, David thought.

Invisible

Wherever he went, people used to recognize him. They were happy to see him. They wanted to be with him. His days were filled with meetings, lunches and dinners. Someone always wanted him for something.

But over time he lost his power and his looks. His calendar, once jam-packed, is now open. No one reaches out to him. No one needs him anymore. No one wants him anymore. When he goes out, no one looks his way. He feels invisible.

Sitting alone, he wonders whatever happened to all those people he no longer sees. Are they too feeling invisible?

Out of Place

I drove down a street I'd walked countless times as a boy, scanning houses that looked vaguely familiar.

Soon I reached the small, red brick house where I'd grown up. I parked in the driveway, walked to the front door and rang the bell, but no one was home.

I looked around. The trim color, the porch light, the front door were all different. The trees in the front yard were huge. When my father planted them, they were saplings.

All of a sudden, I felt out of place, like I didn't belong there.

I took off and never went back.

If Only

If only I had known you, but you came and left so quickly.

Would we have gone to baseball games or father-daughter dances? How did you look? Whose image was borne in your face?

In your short life, did you know you were loved? Did you feel our prayers? Did you know the joy you enkindled?

Why did you have to go so soon? Was some flaw of mine at fault? Or did you live your life in full, as it was meant to be?

Will we meet one day? Can I hold you then and kiss you?

Discovery

Eye of the Storm

Scanning news headlines, Dylan felt his chest tighten. Mass shootings, war, Covid surges, protests, violent crime, stagflation, extreme weather events. The bad news never stopped. For Dylan, the world had become a dizzying maelstrom.

Dylan closed his laptop and thought about his life. His grass needed cutting. His car needed new brakes. His wife seemed distant.

Dylan made an appointment with an auto repair shop, then went outside and mowed his lawn. That evening, he took his wife to dinner.

The next morning, Dylan was about to open his laptop. But instead, he closed his eyes and stilled his mind.

Soothe Your Soul

Rick's mother had been blind for 20 years, but that hadn't kept his parents from riding their tandem bike. Now, though, his father was gone.

"Is there anything else I can do for you, Mom?" Rick said as he got ready to leave for home after the funeral.

"You can go on a bike ride with me sometime."

"Okay. I'll be back in two weeks."

Two weeks later, Rick returned. He went out to the garage and pulled out his father's car. He had mounted a bike rack on the roof. Rick struggled to get the big bike up there. He wondered how his father had done it.

"Ready to go, Mom?"

"Absolutely," she said with a smile.

Riding along a trail with his mother behind him, Rick remembered his father taking him for bike rides and hikes through these woods when he was a kid. Rick had loved the woods. But he hadn't spent time in nature in many years. He was always working.

He remembered his father talking reverently about nature.

"It soothes your soul," he used to say.

But as soon as Rick moved away, he got busy. He stayed busy and never made time to take his own children on bike rides or hikes.

He lost touch with the Earth. Now the sights and smells and sounds of the woods were all around him, and he felt something deep inside he'd nearly forgotten.

Rick thought of his father and smiled. He could almost hear his voice when his mother said, "Isn't it beautiful, Richard?"

"Yeah, Mom, it is."

Something

She was stunning. Wherever she went, every eye was on her. His looks were passable at best.

But she saw something in him, something endearing, something that made her want to be with him.

Her friends couldn't understand.

"Is she crazy?" one whispered.

"She can do so much better," said another.

But she loved him and, seeing that, her friends put aside their judgment, opened their hearts and began to glimpse something of what she saw in him.

New Way

The main road near his house was closed for eight weeks.

"Damn," he said when he first saw the sign. The detour would take him an extra 10 minutes.

On the new route, he saw things he hadn't noticed: mid-century modern homes, walking paths, a playground. It was like discovering a new world.

He tried doing other things differently: brushing his teeth with his left hand, washing his body before his hair in the shower, brewing coffee with a slow-drip machine. All of a sudden, he had to pay attention.

His life had become old. Now it began to feel new again.

Addicted

Jennifer had long been filled with a sense of her own self-importance, but her cell phone made her feel indispensable.

Her husband, feeling ignored, offered her $1,000 to give up her phone for one day. Feeling chastened, she handed it over.

They worked at home in adjoining rooms. Through the day, Jennifer could hear her phone beeping, buzzing and ringing. It was driving her crazy.

Finally, after three calls in a row, Jennifer could take no more. She burst into the next room, grabbed her phone and looked to see who'd been trying so hard to reach her.

Spam.

Back to Business

Countless companies adopted virtue signaling, the practice of showing their moral correctness on a range of social issues, from sustainability to diversity. Most did it to burnish their brands and hold onto woke employees.

But then politicians, activists and those woke employees began to pressure companies to take stands on contentious, real-world issues. Companies became embroiled in controversies, pissing off their customers, shareholders and "unwoke" employees. What was once a halo over their heads had become a millstone around their necks.

So CEOs pulled back from social issues and got back to business. Social activists looked for new allies.

Seeds

Both were in bunkers. One by choice. The other by force.

One sought to slaughter innocents. The other sought to protect them.

One spun lies. The other spoke truth.

One was self-absorbed. The other self-aware.

One wielded power. The other asked for help.

One ordered his troops to attack. The other called on his people to defend.

One longed for yesterday. The other cherished today.

One cast a shadow. The other shone a light.

Inside each of them were seeds, the seeds that lay dormant inside each of us. Like them, we choose which seeds to water.

Two Worlds

He'd begun walking every day on a trail that runs along a river. He viewed the river with mixed emotions because he had always been both drawn to the water and wary of it.

One summer day, he left the trail and went down to the river. He stood on the bank and watched the water ripple and shimmer in the sunlight. It was mesmerizing.

He sat down, took off one shoe and sock and put his foot in the water. At first, the cold water stung, but then it felt good, and he took off his other shoe and sock and sat with his feet in the shallow water.

The water cooled him. After a while, though, looking out at some rapids, he began to grow uneasy and got out.

The following day was steamy. On his walk, he heard laughter and splashing. Through the trees, he could see a group of young people playing on the other side of the river. He envied them. He'd never had such an experience because he couldn't swim.

But as the sun beat down, the cool water beckoned him, and he went down to the river again. This time, as joyful cries of youth echoed across the water, he took off his shoes and socks, pulled up his pant legs and slowly waded in.

At first, the water felt invigorating. But the current was stronger and the water suddenly deeper than he had expected, and he lost his balance and fell in.

The current carried him downstream. Fortunately, he was able to grab onto a partially submerged tree limb and pull himself to shore.

As he climbed the bank, soaked and shaking, he swore he would never go near the water again. I was nearly lost, he thought.

But a week or so later, he was drawn back to the river. He sat on the bank and once again slipped his bare feet into the water.

He took a deep breath. Sitting still, with the familiar Earth beneath him and the mysterious river before him, he began to know the peace of living in two worlds.

Eyes

They'd seen each other in passing or online for nearly two years but not without masks. They'd never met. But in the quiet of their young hearts, they were attracted to one another.

Never mind her braces or his zits. They'd always liked each other's eyes. Their masks had only intensified that attraction.

The first day masks were no longer required at school, they spotted each other in the hallway, as usual, changing classes. This time, though, as they drew close, her bright smile and his handsome, clean-shaven face brought them to a stop.

"Hi," they said in unison.

Stay

Ben had fought in a "forever war" for 20 years when the US finally pulled out. He had passed up nearly two dozen chances to end his tour and go home. Not that he cared for the conflict. He stayed because he incurred a great debt in that faraway land and he felt duty-bound to repay it.

Ben was an only child, the son of an abusive father and a mother he couldn't remember. She vanished when he was three. No one knew why.

For the next two years, Ben had a host of "mothers," women who also lived in the trailer park. They kept an eye on Ben while his father was at work. On average, that was about three days a week. For Ben, those were the good days, when he was beyond his father's reach.

The surrogate mothering stopped, though, when Ben turned five and started kindergarten.

"If you're old enough to go to school, you're old enough to fend for yourself," his father said.

Ben took a bus to and from school. Some mornings, his father was still asleep when Ben left. When Ben got home, his father was usually gone or passed out.

That was the routine all through grade school. By the time he was in high school, Ben started drinking. One night, he came home drunk, and his father cursed at him. Ben cursed back. His father came at him, but Ben, who was now as tall as his father, slugged him in the jaw and knocked him out. After that, Ben's father never laid a hand on him again.

On his eighteenth birthday, Ben enlisted in the Army. He took a train to Fort Benning in Georgia. His father didn't even say goodbye. Ben spent 10 weeks in basic training, then shipped out to Afghanistan.

Maybe Ben didn't hear the command. Or maybe it was because he wasn't used to being on defense. Or maybe it was just because he was still green. But he got separated from his unit, which came under attack in a small town.

Ben huddled behind a stone wall near a small house. Peeking over, he saw a group of soldiers advancing up the hill. For a moment, he was tempted to fire down on them. But then he remembered he was alone and realized that would be suicide.

"In here," said a small voice behind him.

Ben wheeled around. A small girl stood in the doorway of the house. A man and a woman stared out from behind her.

"Hide in here," the girl said.

Ben heard gunfire. It was coming from the town, from others in his unit, he suspected. Then he heard the soldiers just below returning fire. They were getting closer.

He knew he had to find cover. He didn't know what might lay waiting inside the house, but he was willing to risk it. Staying low, he made a break for the open door.

When he was inside, the girl shut the door behind him. Ben looked around, his rifle still at the ready. The girl who had let him in had backed up against the man, who put his arms around her. A small boy, smaller than the girl, stood with his back to the woman.

The man said something in Pashto, which Ben didn't understand. The girl looked up at the man and said something in Pashto too. He looked at her and nodded.

"Hide here," she said to Ben, stepping quickly to the middle of the room.

The man and woman followed her. They grabbed opposite ends of a rug and slid it across the wooden floor, revealing a small trap door. The man pulled back the door, looked up at Ben and pointed down.

"Hide here," the girl said.

Ben stepped over to the opening in the floor and looked down into it. He could see a ladder but nothing beyond that. Outside the sound of gunfire was growing louder. Realizing he had no other choice, Ben climbed down the ladder until he reached a dirt floor. Someone closed the trap door above him, leaving him standing in total darkness.

He heard footsteps above and the rug being dragged across the floor. He heard chairs being scooted, then low talking, then silence.

He heard a door swing open hard, then men's voices. They were all speaking in Pashto, their voices rising. Heavy footsteps thundered around the room above him. He heard chairs being scooted again.

Then he heard a man yelling. Then another man yelling. Then gunfire and screams. Then thuds. Then no more screams. Then heavy footsteps. Then men's voices. Then a door creak open. Then voices trailing off. Then nothing.

Ben waited in the cool darkness for what seemed like a long time, his heart pounding, until he was sure the soldiers were gone.

He climbed the ladder and slowly pushed the trap door up slightly. He peered out but could see nothing because the rug was covering the door. He pushed the door open all the way, but the rug still covered it. He made his way up the ladder and pushed the rug aside.

He looked around and saw the bodies of the man, the woman and the children lying on the floor, blood seeping out from beneath them.

The door was open. He stepped over to it, gripping his rifle. He looked around. Seeing no one, he shut the door.

He went to the woman and knelt beside her. No pulse. Then the man. No pulse. Then the boy. No pulse. Then the girl. When he put his fingers on her neck, she moved slightly and moaned.

She was covered with blood. He slung his rifle over his shoulder and scooped her up. She opened her eyes and cried out.

"It's okay," he said. "I've got you."

He managed to open the door while holding the girl, then went out to find his unit.

Her name was Sadia. She was eight years old. During her operation at a field hospital, Ben waited, nervously pacing outside. Between maneuvers, he visited her there during her long recovery.

Without her father, mother and brother, Sadia had no one. So Ben sort of adopted her. He managed to stay near her and care for her throughout his first tour. Then he re-upped so he could continue to care for her.

He fed her, clothed her and gave her shelter. She called him Papa and gave him her heart.

Through the years, Ben watched Sadia grow up. He watched her fall in love and get married. He watched her have children and care for them lovingly. Sadia taught them to call him Papa too. He became their Papa, and they became his family.

It was a most unorthodox arrangement. But Ben's commanding officers knew the back story. They always cut him slack, and for 20 years he was a reliable pair of boots on the ground.

. . .

When the US decided to pull its troops out of Afghanistan, Ben was torn. Should he go home or stay in the place which had become his home?

"Stay with us, Papa," Sadia said.

He looked at her and thought of the first time he'd seen her. "Hide here," she said. They had saved one another. But not just that. Because of her, he became the father he had never known. Because of him, she became the mother he could not remember.

Ben was honorably discharged. He handed in his rifle, gathered in his family and stayed.

Bend

As a boy, Nick lived near a woods thick with pine trees, tall and broad.

Nick and his friends climbed them, grasping and stepping up sturdy branches like ladder rungs. The boys were light, but when they neared the treetops, the soft wood began to bend. Up high, the trunks were thin but strong and flexible too.

The boys would throw their weight, the trees would sway back and forth like upside-down pendulums and the boys would hold tight, swinging wildly, sometimes nearly touching the ground.

Years later, Nick wrote a bestseller called *The Power of Agility*.

New Neighbor

Linda Williams turned off her TV. Another fatal shooting involving an illegal immigrant. It had taken place 50 miles away, but the news still put Linda on edge. Illegals seemed to be everywhere these days.

Linda lived alone. She had a home security system but still felt vulnerable. Her neighborhood had been idyllic when she and her late husband Jim raised their kids. Now there were all kinds of people living there.

Just a few weeks earlier, a strange-looking family had moved in two doors down. Linda hadn't met them, but she could tell they were immigrants by the way they dressed. Maybe they too were illegals, she thought.

It was a warm, sunny morning, and Linda decided to take a walk. She put on a wide brim hat, locked her front door and headed out.

Walking down the sidewalk, she came upon a young woman and a little girl kicking a ball back and forth in the front yard of the new neighbors' house.

"Good morning," the young woman said.

Linda said nothing. The woman just smiled and kicked the ball to the girl, but it bounced by her. It rolled between two parked cars and into the street. The girl ran after it.

"Layla!" the woman screamed.

Linda saw a car coming. She bolted after the child, who started to squeeze through the parked cars. Linda grabbed her by the shirt and yanked her back. They both fell backward into the grass.

The young woman hurried over, dropped to her knees and gathered the girl in. The woman was crying and saying something Linda didn't understand.

"Is she okay?" Linda said, slowly getting to her feet.

But the woman didn't answer. Instead, she picked up the girl and carried her into the house.

Linda brushed off her pants, put her hat back on and resumed her walk. She wondered where the woman and the girl were from and what language the woman had been speaking. She hoped the girl was okay.

Back home, eating lunch, Linda heard a knock at her front door. She opened it. On her porch stood the woman and the girl. The woman was holding a plate full of pastries.

"My name is Amara," she said, "and this is Layla."

The girl looked up at Linda and smiled.

"I'm Linda."

"Hello, Linda," Amara said. "Thank you for my daughter."

Let Go

Glancing at the latest headlines, Nick felt his heart race. The news was overwhelming. War, famine, inflation, protests, shootings, droughts, wildfires, viruses. Closer to home, his mother lay dying, his job was on the line and a fierce storm had just toppled a big maple tree in his backyard.

Nick was breathing hard. He felt dizzy. He had to sit down.

He closed his eyes and envisioned the troubles all around him, all the things that gripped him and were pulling him down. Then, one by one, Nick let them go, and they let go of him.

Lesson

He'd been trying to teach his teenage son Alex something about being a man. He told him about doing the right thing, treating others with respect and taking responsibility.

But Alex thought his father was naive. He knew leaders lie, people trash each other on social media and criminals get off scot-free.

One day, Alex called his mother a bitch. She began to cry and sent her son to his room.

When his father got home, he went up to Alex's room. He knocked and went in. He looked defeated. He said nothing.

Pained by hurting his mother and disappointing his father, Alex burst into tears.

Observe

He felt angry. He still wasn't sure why he'd been sent to this faraway land. None of his colleagues had ever been given a "broadening assignment." Did he have some deficit? If so, wasn't there an easier way to get training?

He didn't know how to eat the unfamiliar food in front of him. He watched others in the crowded restaurant. He listened more carefully. He didn't know their language, but he began to get a sense of what they were saying from their facial expressions and tone of voice. He started paying closer attention to everything and everyone around him.

Awkwardly holding his chopsticks, he slowly brought the food to his mouth.

The Work

Bernard lived to work. Over the holidays, he never stopped going into the office, even though his employees had two weeks off. He considered them soft.

"Who's there?" he said, looking up from his desk.

A small woman appeared at his door.

"Excuse me, sir," she said with a heavy accent. "I am here for your trash."

"Okay. Come in."

She hurried across the room and quietly emptied his small, brass trash can.

"You work on Christmas Day?" Bernard said.

"Yes. I work every day."

Lying in bed that night, Bernard wondered if, unlike him, the woman had a family.

Pivot Points

Aaron was once a righteous man, but he lost his way. He gave into temptation. He sinned. His life became a series of new lows.

In time, Aaron felt guilty for what he had done. He was ashamed. He atoned for his sins and changed his ways.

Looking back, Aaron realized his low points had become pivot points. The scars on his soul were where his spirit had been mended. The broken places had given rise to his renewal.

Fantasy

New Beginning

April 2470

I should have started this journal sooner so there would be some record of the final days of our species. But how was I to know I would be among the last?

If we don't make it, I hope there will be other life forms after us that can read. If they read this, maybe they'll make better choices than we have.

My name is Novelia. It means "new one." My parents told me they chose that name because by 2432, the year I was born, there were so few births.

They hoped I might represent a new beginning. But by the time they died, my parents had lost hope.

. . .

We've been walking for about a month. We're somewhere in Pennsylvania, heading for Chicago. We've heard there's a colony there.

For the most part, we walk along old roads. Some are barely visible, with trees and whole fields grown up through the crumbling pavement. Occasionally, we come upon the rusted shell of an old car.

There are four of us, two pair bonds: Aliyah and Santiago and Andrew and me. Andrew and I have been together for six months. That's the longest I've been with a man.

My parents were a pair bond too. They were together for 20 years. My mother told me I kept them together. But I think she loved my father, and I think he loved her.

People used to fall in love and get married — in churches. Now no one gets married, and churches have either fallen into ruins or been hollowed out, their pews used for firewood.

And these days, love is no use.

My great grandparents went to school. I can't even imagine it. The last schools were closed a century ago. There weren't enough children, and education was no longer a priority. Teachers died off, and no one took their place.

I was lucky. My great grandmother believed it was important that her daughter, my grandmother, learn to read and write, and so she taught her at home. My grandmother did the same thing with my mother, who did the same with me.

None of these women talked much about it because, more and more, reading and writing were viewed with suspicion. Books and the internet were filled with new ideas, and it was new ideas that got us into this mess.

But it's a moot point now because books and the internet are long gone.

.   .   .

Who knows how many of us are left. I mean in the world.

The last official estimates go back a century. At that point, the world's population had dropped to around one billion. Since then, the rate of decline has been even steeper. I doubt there are even a few million people left on Earth.

We may well go extinct. How did we get to this point?

Climate change. The rejection of technology. The biggest reason, though, has to be that we've nearly stopped reproducing.

That trend started more than 300 years ago. Since then, the population has aged dramatically, and deaths have greatly outnumbered births. Without health care, most people these days don't make it to 40.

I've long dreamed of having a baby. But like most men, Andrew is sterile, and I'm almost 40.

Our days are long, framed by the sun. We live in pairs and pods. Wild animals of all sorts now roam free. We have no guns. Spears, knives and bows and arrows are our only defense.

I do hope we make it to Chicago. Not knowing how long it might take us, we waited until spring to leave New York. The nights are chilly. We huddle together.

But the days are warm, and we've found great fields of winter wheat and rivers and lakes teeming with fish, so we're getting enough to eat.

Life is lonely. I have no friends. Meeting Andrew was such a pleasant surprise. He is much more than a friend.

The first time I saw Andrew, I noticed he wasn't carrying a bow. I asked him why. He told me he doesn't kill animals for food. He said he doesn't believe it's right.

Andrew told me he wants to marry me. I asked him why. He said he wants God to join us.

How refreshing to meet someone so kind, someone who still believes in God.

Andrew tells me he loves me. I had almost forgotten about love. Now that I'm in love, though, it makes me want to live.

I wish we still had medicines. Lately, I've felt nauseous. My belly's been bloated too. I've lost track of my time of the month.

Am I sick? Maybe I'm nearing the end of my life. I don't know. I hope I'm not dying.

The sun is rising. When we got here last night it was dark. We camped under some trees for protection. Now I can see we're in a grove of cherry trees. The sweet fragrance of pink and white blossoms fills the cool morning air.

Andrew is still asleep beside me. The cloudless blue sky looks so pure. Beyond the trees, a green meadow with white, red and yellow wildflowers stretches for as far as I can see. I hear birds singing. I do believe the Earth is healing.

I look around and see the skyline of a city in the distance. I see smoke rising and tall buildings. This must be Chicago.

I stand up. I feel something move within me, a sensation I've never felt before. Could I be pregnant? I am overwhelmed by the very idea.

I am trembling. My heart is racing. My legs feel weak. I sit back down. Something, or someone, inside me is moving again.

I must be pregnant. But how can that be? I don't know. It must be a miracle.

I wonder if it's a boy or a girl. I begin to cry. I hope I live to see my child grow up. I hope I am part of a new beginning.

The Tailor

He made clothing with the precision of a great craftsman, but his aim was not pure.

Each garment he fashioned featured one thread which, if pulled, would cause the whole thing to fall apart. He carefully left the tiniest end of it protruding.

He didn't think much of his customers, though he was happy to take their money. Fortunately, most never noticed the frayed ends on their stylish new clothes.

As winter approached, the tailor made himself an elegant overcoat. One day, he noticed a stray thread on his sleeve. Instinctively, he pulled it, then stood shivering in the cold.

Mrs. Hamilton

When you're a kid, all grown-ups are a little mysterious. When I was a kid, Mrs. Hamilton, who lived next door, was the most mysterious grown-up of all.

For starters, no one knew where she came from. One day, she just showed up. Everyone called her Mrs. Hamilton, but we never saw her husband or any children. There were rumors, though.

We always knew when Mrs. Hamilton was around because she cackled. She cackled loudly and often.

Mrs. Hamilton always made you think of Halloween. She had stringy hair, a long nose, beady eyes, greenish skin, even a wart on her chin. She was tall and thin. She wore long dresses and floppy hats.

We usually saw her at dusk, walking around her yard. Sometimes she sat on a bench under a sycamore tree in her backyard with a big black cat at her side. She never spoke to us, and we never had the courage to approach her.

"Mrs. Hamilton looks like a witch," my sister said at dinner one night.

"Sarah!" my mother scolded.

"Well, she does," my father murmured.

"Jack!" said my mother, biting her lip.

One Halloween, I was the last one home after trick-or-treating. I always tried to get as much candy as I could.

As I stepped onto our front porch, I heard a familiar cackle. It was louder than ever, though. I looked over at Mrs. Hamilton's house, which strangely had been dark the whole evening.

I saw a figure rising above the roof. It looked like a woman riding a broomstick. Her robe flapped wildly behind her. She flew in ascending, widening circles, her cackling ever fainter. Then she rode across the wondrously bright full moon and into the murky darkness beyond.

I never saw Mrs. Hamilton again.

Light

Angels

A mother holds her infant son to her breast, hoping her malnourished body can sustain this precious new life.

A father dips a ladle into a bucket of water he has strained to lift from a deep well and hands it to his thirsty daughter.

A grandmother gathers her young grandchildren close to shield them from the thunder of missiles overhead and, through the warmth of her body, give them comfort.

This Christmas, there are angels in Burundi, Argentina and Ukraine. There are angels everywhere. They guard the light.

Reconstruction

Five months after the end of a war that pitted brother against brother, still dressed in his blue uniform, Thomas Fenwick approached a brick house surrounded by oaks and maples with leaves of red and brown. White chickens roamed free in the long, dewy grass, pecking at insects. Through the front window, Thomas spotted an anxious, lovely face.

"Cover me," he said to his two fellow horsemen as he dismounted.

His eyes fixed on the face in that window, his vision sharpened by years of combat, Thomas pulled his rifle from the leather scabbard below his saddle. He slowly walked the fieldstone path to the broad, wooden porch. All the while, the young woman in the window remained still, watching him.

Thomas ascended the steps and strode to the front door. Floorboards creaked. He removed his cap. Long, brown hair tucked underneath fell down to his shoulders. He raised his right hand and gently knocked on the weathered oak door.

Thomas heard footsteps inside, coming closer. He gripped the barrel of his rifle more tightly. After months of pacifying Southerners, he had learned to be wary.

He heard metal slide on the other side of the door. Then the door slowly opened. Inside stood the young woman. She was petite and looked even lovelier up close. Her eyes were blue. Her chestnut hair was parted in the middle and pulled back into a braided bun behind her head. She wore a long, gray dress. Beside her, holding her hand, stood a little boy.

"Yes?" she said softly.

"Good morning, ma'am. My name is Thomas Fenwick. I am a captain in the Union Army. My men and I are on our way through Tennessee to make sure everyone is okay."

She stared at him, as if she expected him to say more.

Finally, he said, "Is everyone here okay?"

She blinked.

"Yes, we are holding up."

"I'm glad to hear that. Would you mind if I looked around?"

She looked puzzled.

"It's standard procedure."

"All right."

Thomas, still on the porch, turned to his men and said, "Why don't you go ahead? I'll secure this one and catch up."

One of the men grinned. Thomas heard a gasp behind him and turned back around. The woman was holding her hand to her mouth. Her eyes were wide. She looked frightened.

"It's okay," he said. "I won't harm you. There's nothing to fear."

The two horsemen turned and rode away.

"Come in," the woman said tentatively.

Thomas stepped inside and shut the door behind him. After years of living out of a tent, he was still getting used to being in real homes again.

"My name is Maggie Calhoun," the woman said. "And this is my son, Luke."

"It's a pleasure to meet you, Mrs. Calhoun," Thomas said, extending his hand.

She looked surprised but took it. Hers was the smallest hand and the softest skin Thomas had felt in a long time.

He then said, "Hello, Luke," again extending his hand. But the boy retreated behind his mother.

"You're welcome to look around," Maggie said. "We have an upstairs and a cellar. Out back, there's a barn and three cabins."

"Cabins?"

"For the slaves. They're all gone now, of course."

"Is your husband here?"

"No."

"Where is he?"

"He's dead."

"I'm sorry."

"Thank you. Would you like some coffee, captain? I just made some, fresh."

"I'd love some."

"I'll be right back. Please have a seat," she said, nodding toward the parlor.

She left with Luke holding fast to her hand.

Thomas stepped into the parlor and sat down in a high-backed armchair near the fireplace. He was still getting used to sitting on soft surfaces again too.

He put his cap on his lap and set his rifle next to him on the floor. He looked around the sunlit room and took in the sweet, earthy aroma of good coffee and was reminded of home.

A few minutes later, Maggie came back, carefully balancing two white, porcelain cups on saucers, with Luke still at her side. Thomas got up and took one of the cups.

"Thank you," he said.

Turning to Luke, Maggie said, "Why don't you go upstairs for a few minutes while I talk with Captain Fenwick?"

"Yes, Mother," he said.

Maggie sat down on the sofa across from Thomas.

"You've got a very good boy there," he said.

"Thank you. Luke is an angel."

They sipped their coffees. It was by far the best coffee Thomas had had in years. He'd grown accustomed to drinking chicory but never liked it.

"If I may be so bold, was your husband in the war?"

"Yes, he fought for our side. He was killed at Cumberland Gap."

"I'm sorry. So you and the boy have been alone here ever since?"

"No. My daughter died last winter, and the slaves all left soon after Appomattox."

"What was your daughter's name?"

"Her name was Emily."

"How old was she?"

"Just two."

"I'm sorry you've had to endure so much loss."

Maggie simply nodded.

"I noticed crops in your fields," he said, changing the subject.

"Yes, cotton and tobacco. They were planted in the spring."

"Is there anyone to harvest them?"

"Just me, I'm afraid. I tried to cut tobacco leaves, but I didn't get very far. The tobacco still out in the fields is dead. The cotton is about ripe. I'll pick what I can, but I reckon I won't get very far on that either."

"What will you do? How will you get by?"

"I've decided I'll have to sell this place."

"Where will you go?"

"I'll move back home and live with my sister and her family."

"Where's home?"

"Lexington."

He nodded.

"Have you been there?"

"Yes. Not long ago, in fact."

Her face softened. She sipped her coffee, studying him over the rim of her cup.

"Where are you from?" she said.

"Just outside of Philadelphia."

"You're a long way from home."

"Yes."

"How long have you been in the Army?"

"Since sixty-one. I joined right after Sumpter."

"If I may ask, why?"

"I've always believed slavery is wrong. Our cause was just. I wanted to help free the slaves."

"Well, they're free now."

"Thank God."

"So why have you stayed on?"

"To help finish up."

"But don't you want to go home?"

"I'm not sure I'm welcome there any more."

"Why?"

"We're Quakers. We're supposed to be pacifists. When I said I wanted to enlist, my father said, 'We don't fight. We don't kill.' But I signed up anyway. He was livid. I'd never seen him so upset. He told me to get out, that I didn't belong there any more."

"I'm sorry."

Thomas nodded and said nothing.

"Have you written your family?"

"No."

"So they don't know if you're alive? They must be so worried about you."

"I've wanted to write, but ... the things I've done. I've taken men's lives. How could my parents ever understand?"

"But you're their son. They'll never stop loving you."

"I hope you're right. Maybe I will go back one day. Maybe after I finish this tour."

"When will that be?"

"I signed on for three months. I've served five. So I can ask to be discharged whenever I want."

"If you went home, what would you do?"

"My father is a farmer. He grows corn and wheat. I'd probably work on the farm and take it over one day. That is, if he'd take me back."

They had both finished their coffee.

"Your parents must miss you terribly," she said.

He looked away.

"Captain, I have an idea."

"What's that?"

"If you do decide to leave the Army, you could live here, in one of the cabins out back. You could help me pick the cotton, and I could pay you from the money it fetches. After that, you could leave any time you like. You could go home."

He stared at her, trying to comprehend that idea. Just then, he heard someone coming down the stairs. Instinctively, he reached for his rifle.

Luke appeared in the doorway. He looked at Thomas, holding his gun. He darted over to his mother and climbed up next to her on the sofa. He got so close that his left leg was covered by the folds of her dress. She wrapped her arm around him and gently kissed his head.

"It's okay," she whispered.

Thomas remembered his mother holding him and kissing him that way when he was a boy. He longed to be near her again.

He looked at Maggie. The autumn light through the wavy glass window behind her cast a mystical glow.

"Do you make coffee this good *every* morning?"

Good Conscience

I've been with you a long time. I am your foundation and your guide. I show you the right path, though you choose which path you'll take.

When you follow the right path, we are whole. When you deviate, I miss you, as a parent misses an absent child.

Yet I know it is only by exploring that you can find your own way. And only then am I expanded, even as you are deepened.

I know you will go astray. Know that when you do, no matter how late the hour, I will be waiting to welcome you home.

My Name is Francis

He'd been an Olympian. His name was Francis, but his coach called him Frank. Francis sounded too soft.

After the Olympics, he moved back to the small town where he'd grown up. He kept a low profile. His fame faded. His wife left him.

He ran into a neighbor in a coffee shop. They hadn't met, but he knew she lived alone. He asked if she'd like to sit down. She said yes.

"This is awkward," she said, "but I can't recall your name."

"My name is Francis, but people call me Frank."

"I'd like to call you Francis."

First Day

He remembered his first day of first grade like it was yesterday. He was filled with excitement.

He felt that way 30 years later when he walked his daughter to school on her first day.

He felt that way 60 years later when he walked his grandson to school on his first day.

And he felt that way 90 years later as his grandson pushed him to school on his great granddaughter's first day.

For a moment, he was wistful. But then he smiled, feeling grateful for all those first days and excited that he still had one more ahead.

Fat Pat

Fat Pat. That's what everyone called him. Kids can be cruel.

Growing up, Pat had only one friend, a kid named Bill.

At high school graduation, Pat couldn't make it up the steps to the stage to get his diploma, so the principal brought it down. Pat felt humiliated.

That evening, when everybody else was partying, Bill said, "Let's go for a walk."

Pat enjoyed it so much that he began walking on his own every day. With every step, he felt more hopeful.

Now, 20 years later, Bill is an exercise physiologist, and Pat runs marathons.

Prayer

I followed a trail through whispering beachgrass down to the shore. The soft glow of the just-rising sun lighted my way.

I stepped across the cool sand to the water's edge. I sat and watched the sun slowly rise. Seabirds glided gracefully. Small waves lapped at my feet.

When did my life become so frantic? When did living become a chore? When did I lose my way?

I closed my eyes, breathed in the warm air and prayed that my heart return to the rhythm of the sea.

An Ordinary Day

It was a Wednesday.

I'd given up on kindness. The world had become harsh. People casting stones. People living unto themselves. People, once loving, now indifferent.

And I'd begun feeling vindictive, closed and apathetic too.

I was waiting in the checkout line at the grocery. My cart was full. You were carrying a couple of items. I let you go ahead.

"Thank you," you said with a smile.

My groceries bagged, I went to pay, but the cashier said you'd taken care of my bill.

The world changed that day. I changed that day. It was a Wednesday.

Open Arms

It was another lonely, dreary day online.

Through his bedroom window, someone walking in the cul-de-sac caught Jacob's eye. It was Madison. Jacob's heart beat faster.

He and Madison were close as children, but she'd become one of the cool kids. They hadn't seen each other in person in a long time.

Wasn't Madison in class this morning? Jacob looked down at his screen. She wasn't there. His gaze shot back to the street. There she was, walking alone.

Jacob got up, made his way past rooms where his parents were on Zoom calls and slipped out the front door.

As kids, Jacob and Madison ran to each other, so happy to see one another. Now he ran to catch up with her. She heard his footsteps and turned around.

"Hey, Maddie," he said, slowing to a walk.

"Hey, Jake," she said with a smile and open arms.

Appreciation

She browsed the artwork around the room where her painting was newly hung. She considered this painting her finest work, and she was eager to see the other museumgoers' reactions.

But people gave it only a passing glance. As they walked by it, her heart sank.

She sat down on a bench in the middle of the room. She watched a young man approach her painting. He stopped and studied it. After a few minutes, he slowly backed away and sat beside her, his eyes still fixed on her creation.

He sat there silently, then whispered, "That speaks to me."

Beginning

Rob was a sweet, quiet, sensitive boy. He was bullied at school, and his parents were hard on him at home. These experiences wounded him but steeled him too.

He took a liking to blue jays. Nobody messed with them, not even the bigger birds.

Rob began to think of himself as a blue jay. He became mean and aggressive, and people backed off.

Now, after a lifetime of intimidating others, Rob lay dying. He expected to hear the familiar screech of blue jays through his open window. Instead, the gentle coo of a mourning dove called him back to his beginning.

Giveaway

He had worked tirelessly to improve his situation. He had sacrificed much. But he did what it took to acquire great wealth, gain stature and bury the memory of his poor childhood.

Now, though, his memories arose like spirits, and he was pained by the remembrance of how he had left others behind and shared none of his treasure.

As the holidays approached, filled with shame, he began giving away his possessions. Until his house was empty. Until he was empty. Until he had been made low and his heart was opened and he was ready to receive once again.

Mercy

He trudged through the snowy field to the woods where he had cut down an evergreen every Christmas for decades.

His kids used to go with him. Each would find a favorite and plead with him to make it their family Christmas tree that year. He gave them all a turn.

This year everyone had been felled by the virus or was in quarantine. Only he would see the Christmas tree.

At the edge of the woods, he stopped. In the silence, he listened to the wind. In the wind, he heard pleas for mercy.

His axe still on his shoulder, he turned around and headed back home.

My Gift

I'd just finished Christmas shopping and was heading out of downtown when my car broke down.

Waiting for AAA, I saw a man, wrapped in a blanket, sitting on the sidewalk. His bare hands were cupped over his mouth. His breath rolled through his fingers and rose in little misty clouds in the frigid air.

I'd been shopping for gifts for my loved ones. I'd even bought myself a coat.

I watched the man on the sidewalk pull his blanket more tightly around himself.

I grabbed my new coat from my backseat and got out.

"Merry Christmas," I said.

To the Rescue

During the pandemic, restaurants, hotels and theaters had to close. Then, with the vaccines, places began to open up again.

But not for long. Workers quit or simply didn't come back. Jobs everywhere went unfilled.

Employers offered greater pay, but it didn't work. People had begun to rethink their lives. Many decided work was no longer a top priority.

But everyone still needed food, shelter and clothing. Who would provide such basics?

Out of desperation, borders were opened, and immigrants came to the rescue, first as laborers, then as business owners. Eventually, they hired the sons and daughters of the unemployed.

Last Day

Marie shivered in the cold as she waited for her bus in the fading light.

It was Christmas Eve, but for Marie, it was still a workday, the last of her long career.

She had lived a solitary life, devoid of much kindness, owing, she had always felt, to her awkward looks.

Her bus arrived. As the doors opened, Marie looked up, expecting to see Sam. But a bearded stranger sat in his place.

Just then, a gust of wind nearly blew Marie over. The driver hurried down the steps.

"Evening, ma'am," he said warmly, taking her by the hand.

Pre-Med

Most students at the Roycemore School in Evanston, Illinois came from money. For the most part, their fathers and a few of their mothers were professionals, but the country was still in the midst of a Great Depression. People made do with what they had. Even the wealthier households had only one car. The Andersons were no exception.

John Anderson took the bus to and from Roycemore. It picked him up and dropped him off about a half mile from his house. Sometimes he walked that stretch alone. Most days, though, he joined other kids, and they walked it together.

One bitterly cold day, in his sophomore year, John got off the bus with two girls. They lived a few streets over. John didn't know them, but he knew they were sisters and that one was a freshman and the other a junior.

John followed them off at their stop. They were walking fast along the side of the street, about 10 paces ahead of him, when he saw the younger girl slip on a patch of black ice. Her feet went out from under her and her books went flying, her arms flailing in the air.

Her body twisted, and she came down on her right leg. John heard something snap. Then he heard the girl cry out in pain.

She landed face down on the ground. Her sister yelled "Helen!" and knelt beside her. She looked around and saw John.

"Help us," she said.

John hurried over. He didn't know what to do. For some reason, he asked himself: what would my father do?

He knelt down and calmly said to the injured girl, "Can you turn over?"

"Yes," she moaned. "I think so."

"Help me turn her," John said to her sister.

The two of them cradled her and gently turned her over on her back. The whole time she was groaning in pain.

"Where does it hurt?" John said.

"My leg."

"Okay," John said. "We'll get help. You're going to be okay. Don't move."

"Okay," the girl said, her voice trembling.

John looked over at the older girl.

"Go to a house and call for help. I'll stay here with your sister."

"Who should I call?"

"I don't know. The police, I guess. We need an ambulance."

"Okay."

She got up and ran to the nearest house.

John looked down at her sister. She was crying and shivering. John took off his wool cap, his scarf and his gloves.

"I'm going to put these under your head, like a pillow," he said.

He slipped his left hand under her head and lifted it slightly. He tucked the articles of clothing, still warm from his body, under her head. Then he took off his coat and draped it over her.

"Better?"

"Much," she said, managing a faint smile. "Thank you."

"You're going to be okay," John said, smiling. "Help is on the way."

She looked up at his face.

"What's your name?"

"John. John Anderson."

"Thank you, John. Thank you for being here."

"You're welcome. What's your name?"

"Helen. Helen Weber."

It was 15 degrees, and the wind was blowing. John was shivering, but he didn't feel the cold. He was completely focused on Helen. He pulled his coat up under her chin and made small talk until Helen's sister returned and an ambulance arrived.

Two men got out and lifted Helen onto a stretcher. Once they secured her with straps, they slid the stretcher inside.

"Can I ride with her?" John said.

The men looked at each other. One of them nodded.

"Okay. Get in."

Helen's sister gathered John's hat, scarf and gloves and handed them to him.

"What's your name?" she said.

"John Anderson."

"Thanks, John. I'm going to run home. I'll ask my mom to call your mom to let her know where you are. Where do you live?"

"Oak Street."

John hopped in the back of the vehicle, squeezing into the small space next to Helen. Both of the ambulance men rode up front.

"There are blankets back there," one of them called back to John. "Put them on her."

"Okay."

He took his coat off Helen and gently placed two blankets over her.

"Warmer?"

"Yes," she said, smiling. "Why don't you put your coat back on? Your lips are blue."

With siren blaring and lights flashing, they sped to Cook County Hospital. On the way, John chatted with Helen about her family, her favorite subjects in school, last Saturday's basketball game — anything to take her mind off her leg.

When they arrived, the ambulance men carefully lifted Helen out. Then John hopped out and followed them to the emergency room.

"Broken right leg," one of the men said to a nurse.

She pulled back the blankets and looked down at Helen's leg.

"Sweetie," she said, "we're going to lift you onto another stretcher."

"Okay," Helen said.

The nurse wheeled a stretcher over, and the men lifted Helen onto it. The movement made her grimace and moan.

"It will be okay," John said, taking her hand.

She looked over at John and squeezed his hand. The nurse released the brake on the stretcher and wheeled Helen away.

John sat alone in the waiting room. He replayed all that had happened, like a movie, in his mind. He thought about Helen. He hoped she would be okay.

Then he heard someone call his name. He looked up. It was his father. He was wearing scrubs. In all the commotion, John had lost track of where he was.

"Dad."

His father stepped over.

"Mom called and told me you were here. Mrs. Weber called her. Her other daughter dropped your books at the house."

John had forgotten about his books.

"What you did today was very brave," his father said.

"It was nothing. I just stayed with her."

"Sometimes, that's the most important thing you can do. I'll be done in about an hour. Wait here. I'll drive you home."

"Okay."

His father got up and started to walk away.

"Dad?"

"Yes?" he said, turning around.

"Is she okay?"

"She's going to be fine. It was a clean break. We're setting it now."

John had always wanted to be a doctor like his father. He was studying biology and chemistry extra hard, knowing they were important for college.

Now, thinking about the look in Helen's eyes as he knelt beside her on the street and rode with her in the ambulance and what his father had just said, John began to think differently about what it means to be a doctor.

The next day, Mrs. Weber brought over a chocolate cake. It had a card with it, addressed to John. He opened it when he got home from school.

Dear John,

Thank you for being with me yesterday. I was really scared, but I got through it because of you. I'll be wearing a cast for a while, but I'll be fine. I'm so glad you were there for me.

Helen

Shadow

Conscripted

The young man looked out the train window, his eyes searching for his parents in the crowd of people waving goodbye to loved ones who, like him, were riding off to war.

He didn't want to go but had little choice. He could have tried to flee. But if he had made it, he might never see his family again. And if he'd been caught, he would have been imprisoned.

Now his parents came into view, but they were not waving or even looking his way. They were holding one another. His mother faced away. His father was crying.

The Abyss

I grew up in a row house on the edge of an old town covered in soot. Our neighborhood bordered woods so dark and deep that they were called The Abyss. Our parents wouldn't let us go in. Rumor had it that a boy who had gone in was never seen again.

By the time I was 10, though, I'd grown tired of playing games in the street. I wanted to explore The Abyss. My friend Mackenzie did too.

One summer morning, we stole into the woods. It was overcast, and under the thick canopy of trees, our eyes strained to see. We followed an overgrown trail and stuck together.

A mile or so in, we came to a big ravine. The trail stopped there. The ravine was wide, and the terrain ascended steeply on both ends.

"What should we do?" Mackenzie said.

"Want to keep going?" I said, hoping she wanted to turn back.

"I guess," she said, peering over the edge.

"Okay," I said. "I'll go first."

I was scared, but I wasn't about to show it. I got down on my belly and scooted back toward the edge.

"Be careful," Mackenzie said, as I began to lower myself down.

The descent was so steep, the ground so loose that I had to hang onto roots. I struggled to find footholds. My arms shook. I had to constantly wipe dirt from my face.

When I was almost down to ground level, I spotted something wedged into a crevasse. The light was quite dim, and I wasn't sure what it was. I leaned in for a closer look.

Now inches from the object, finally realizing what I was looking at, no longer feeling brave, I screamed.

"Cole?" Mackenzie shouted. "What's wrong?"

"Go back!"

"What is it?"

"Go back!" I cried, clambering back up.

I used to love Halloween, but I don't go out anymore. I'm afraid I might see a kid dressed like a skeleton.

Legacy

As a boy, Patrick loved to paint, but his father discouraged him.

"You'll never make any money," he said.

Patrick wanted to study art in college, but his father wouldn't help with tuition unless he majored in business.

Patrick went to work in a coffee shop. He made enough to support himself and painted at night.

One morning, biking to work, Patrick was hit by a car and killed.

He left more than 200 paintings. The art world discovered them, and they sold for a small fortune. In his grief, his father set up a scholarship for art students.

Abandoned

Jonathan was confident and assertive in every part of his life, except for his marriage. Around Tiffany, he was gun-shy.

Just about everything he did anymore made her mad. All he wanted was for her not to be mad at him. He thought about speaking up but kept quiet for fear of making things worse, maybe even much worse. He was afraid she would leave him.

Tiffany had her divorce papers delivered to Jonathan at work. By the time he got home, she was gone.

Cracks

It was a stately home, built long ago by men whose vision was noble and ambitious: to create a place for everyone, where all could live in freedom and happiness. To make sure it would last, the framers fashioned a foundation of great blocks of granite and limestone.

Over the years, the structure was expanded and modernized, but the foundation developed cracks. Unfortunately, those in charge ignored the damage, even as they added costly adornments.

Eventually, the once-mighty base crumbled, bringing the whole house down. Unfriendly neighbors, with their own architects, moved in.

Useful

At the funeral home, Joe and Bob, old friends, shook hands and exchanged pleasantries.

"It's a shame about Dennis," Joe said.

"Yes," said Bob. "What an awful thing."

"The way he died?"

"Yes."

"Well, I guess falling into a widget machine would be a pretty bad way to go," said Joe, keeping his voice low. "But I was really talking about why he was working in that factory at all. I mean he was our age."

"And why was that?"

"When I last saw Dennis, he told me he just wanted to feel useful."

"Yeah," said Bob. "What a shame."

Blue Comet

The old man drove a blue Mercury Comet. It was one of the few things of any value he owned.

They found him slumped over the steering wheel in a parking lot, dead of a heart attack.

He didn't have a will. Both of his daughters wanted his car. They fought for it. When one of them finally got it, the other never spoke to her again.

There is a blue Comet in every family. It can drive a wedge between loved ones.

Hobson's Choice

Hobson was a teenager when he began paying close attention to climate change. What he learned alarmed him.

"Damn!" Hobson said.

He vowed his first car would be electric. When he graduated from college and got a job, Hobson made good on that promise. By then, most cars and trucks were electric.

Hobson felt good about his choice until he heard the news. The mass conversion to electric vehicles was making climate change worse because the power plants supplying all that electricity were spewing even more carbon dioxide and toxic metals into the air.

"Damn!" said Hobson.

The Thing About Low Expectations

Jeremy always had low expectations.

As a boy, he didn't expect anyone to like him. No one did.

As a man, he didn't expect anyone to love him. He lived alone. He didn't expect anyone to hire him. He was self-employed. He didn't expect his neighbors to be friendly. They weren't.

As an old man, he didn't expect anyone to care for him. He died alone.

Jeremy had kept his expectations low so he would never be disappointed. Yet as he lay dying, he realized every day of his life had been filled with disappointment. He hadn't expected that.

Social Media

No one knows exactly when it happened. But at some point, most people became more comfortable communicating on devices than in person.

They'd been emailing and calling for years. Now, though, texting, tweeting, posting and FaceTiming were the preferred modes of communication.

They were efficient, but something was lost. People forgot the feel of shaking hands and embracing. They walked along wooded trails on cell phones, detached from the quiet beauty around them. They no longer saw the unique expression of a face or heard the true tone of a voice.

People were no longer social, but their media were.

The Weeds

It started not with an insult, but the lack of a kind word.

They'd been together a long time. They were sweethearts once. Their conversations were generous and loving.

But over time, they paid less attention to one another. He no longer held the door for her. She no longer noticed when he lost a few pounds. They stopped holding hands.

Maybe they assumed their affection for one another was understood, that close proximity was sufficient, that love would simply last.

But love is a garden. If it's not tended, it will succumb to the weeds. All flowers need care.

Lesson Time

The family had come undone. The children had never been all that close. More of a federation than a union. But over the years, they'd learned to get along.

Now most of the children had left. They were enjoying their freedom. It was their right, of course, but Father never approved.

One of his children, who lived next door, was particularly independent, and he had friends who Father never liked.

Father tried to persuade his son to come back home, but he refused. Father became aggressive, even claiming some of his son's land as his own. The young man resisted at first, but then gave in and learned to live with the encroachment. Father began taunting his son, calling him names, but he simply ignored the old man.

Now Father was enraged. He himself had come undone. He decided it was time for a lesson.

Work

"How was it?" he said.

"Okay," she said.

"Are you tired? You look tired."

"I'm fine."

He sipped his coffee.

"What did you do?"

She opened the fridge and pulled out a can of sparkling water.

"Not much," she said, sitting down across from him. "Orientation mainly."

"Do you think you'll like it?"

"What?"

"Working."

"Yeah, I do."

Then, looking away, she added, "You should try it."

His face turned red. He got up.

"Dinner?" she said.

"I already ate."

He put his coffee cup in the sink, grabbed a beer from the fridge and stepped into the family room.

Asymmetric Warfare

The young man blended in with the crowd of shoppers at the open-air market.

He stopped between the two most popular booths, murmured something and pulled the cord on his vest.

Eleven thousand miles away, a man sat at his desk and leaned closer to his computer screen.

Having located his target, a truck driving north, he moved his cursor over the image and pushed a button on his keyboard.

Technically, asymmetric warfare is one-sided. But to the victims, all war is symmetrical. To the victims, there is no difference between pulling a cord and pushing a button.

Daniel

Daniel was a happy kid until his classmates began calling him fat, so he lost weight.

As a teenager, "Daniel" was no longer cool. A friend suggested he start going by Dan.

In college, Dan majored in art. His roommate told him girls want a guy with prospects, so he switched to business.

After graduation, Dan landed a job, and women finally began to take notice. But when his company let him go, so did his girlfriend.

Dan eked out a living but eventually went broke and found himself in a homeless camp. The others there welcomed him warmly. They called him Daniel.

Fear

I'm all around you. I'm inside you too. I'm in your heart. I'm in your head. I seize you and consume you. I immobilize you. I rob you of reason. I confuse you. I make you weary and bring you down. I make the whole world seem threatening. I fill you with darkness, suspicion and dread. I cause you to hate. You try to hide from me, but I am with you always, like a shadow.

Unless you choose to let me go.

Hunkered Down

At last, it was over. No more deadly virus. No more need for masks. No more forced isolation.

When the pandemic hit, everyone scurried for cover. Life changed overnight. No more working in offices or learning in classrooms. No more going to movies or holiday gatherings. No more travel.

What an adjustment. At first, it was all so stressful. But then people grew accustomed to living online. They grew accustomed to social distancing. They even grew accustomed to solitude.

In the back of their minds, people remembered how crowded and hectic their lives had become before the virus. They were overextended, worn out. So many relationships had become fractious. Entering the world every day was like preparing to do battle.

So now that the pandemic had come to an end, most people stayed put. They had grown safe and secure in their own little worlds. Why run the risks of venturing out again? Living online isn't so bad. Better to stay hunkered down.

Judgment Day

"What did you stand for?"

"Winning."

"Winning?"

"Yes. I built a big business."

"I understand. But what were your guiding principles?"

"Guiding principles?"

"Your core values."

"You mean beyond winning?"

"Yes."

"To do better all the time."

"In what way?"

"Sales and profits."

"Why was that important?"

"It meant I was winning."

Pause.

"I gave a lot of money to charity too."

"Why?"

"Tax deductions. And good PR."

"I can see you're tired," said the interviewer, turning off her recording device. "Why don't we pick it up there tomorrow?"

"Okay," said the old man, closing his eyes one last time.

Price of Ownership

"My songs belong to me," said the aging rock star.

"Thank you, Mr. Clifford," said his attorney.

"Do you have any further questions?" the judge asked the defense attorney.

"No, Your Honor. The defense rests."

The jury found Clifford's former bandmates guilty of copyright infringement. The judge ordered them to pay him nearly a million dollars in damages.

Six months later, Clifford was diagnosed with untreatable throat cancer. No longer able to speak, he wrote his former manager, asking if he would put together a tribute album featuring his best songs, which the band had made famous decades earlier.

"We must decline," his former manager wrote back. "Your songs belong to you."

The Storm

Stepping outside, Jolene was nearly blown over. She went back into her apartment to close her windows.

Driving to work, Jolene felt wind gusts pushing her car back and forth on the road. She gripped her steering wheel more tightly, at times struggling to stay in her lane.

In her office, Jolene looked out and saw trees being whipped around. The sky grew black as night, thunder rattled her building and raindrops strafed her window.

That evening, Jolene drove home at a snail's pace through torrential rain. She wondered what was happening. She didn't know this would be her new normal, that the Earth was angry and could simply take no more.

Demise

Until 200 years ago, humans were all about growth. More wealth. More possessions. More people.

Then came the Great Reckoning, when the Earth could bear no more and humans decided to reverse course.

At last they had begun to come to grips with all the damage they'd done over thousands of years. In a panic, they scaled back dramatically. They stopped acquiring. They stopped developing. They even stopped having children in order to preserve the scarce resources that remained.

But it was too late. After 200,000 years on Earth, humans abruptly vanished, the only species to choose its own demise.

Nostalgia

Small World

Robert awoke early, shuffled down the hall to his kitchen and brewed a cup of coffee.

He sat sipping it and looking out his window. He thought about his life before his world had become so small, about his family, his job and making big decisions, when people looked up to him and treated him with respect.

A truck stopped at the end of his driveway. Robert watched the driver get out and head his way with a package. He wasn't expecting anything.

He hurried to his front door and opened it.

"Good morning, sir," the delivery woman said.

"Good morning!"

Laughter and Tears

Growing up, he got together with his cousins on holidays. They were such happy times, full of music and laughter.

This morning he attended the funeral for one of his cousin's children. "There is a season for everything, a time to every purpose under heaven," read the lector.

After Communion, music played. He closed his eyes and remembered those times as a boy with his cousins. Some who were with him then were with him still.

There is a time for everything. A time for joy and a time for sorrow. A time for laughter and a time for tears.

Sign

My father was a hard man to know. He was quiet, private and stoic. Even in his final days, he never spoke of death. I never knew his mind.

I wish I'd asked him more questions. Did he believe in resurrection? I wish I'd asked him to send me a sign.

When I was a boy, my father used to take me for walks in the woods. He told me we could live in the woods, that everything we needed was there.

I thought of that as I walked through the winter woods the other day, just before I spotted purple, white and yellow crocuses rising through the fallen leaves.

Fun

The Man Who Wouldn't Leave

No one had invited him. He just showed up and acted like he owned the place. He even claimed it was his party.

"But this isn't your house," someone pointed out.

"Says who?" he huffed, sounding like a fourth grader.

He droned on about himself. People tried to avoid him, but he seemed to be everywhere.

Finally, the host had to ask him to leave.

"Excuse me!" he bellowed. "I made this party great. Without me, it's over!"

He grabbed a statuesque woman and left, slamming the door behind them.

Everyone stood still, looking around. Someone laughed. Then everyone laughed, and the party went on.

Night of the Iguana

For Halloween, Garth decided to dress up as Miss Crawly, his grandkids' favorite character from the *Sing* movies.

Grudgingly, his wife Iris helped him on with his costume. Soon Garth was an iguana with pink lipstick, a green cap and a yellow dress.

"Pew! Pew!" Garth said as he passed trick-or-treaters. They laughed. Their parents did too.

Back home, Garth dumped candy and an apple on the kitchen table.

Iris rolled her eyes.

Just then, Garth's right eye fell out and bounced across the floor.

Garth gasped. Then he grabbed the apple and stuck it in its place.

Leaks

John touched a dark spot on his family room ceiling. It was wet.

A plumber replaced a pipe in the upstairs bathroom, a drywall guy patched the ceiling and a painter made it look like new.

A week later, rainwater poured through a cracked skylight. A window guy replaced it. Fixing the damage inside was pricey.

Then John's basement flooded. He didn't have flood insurance, so he had to pay for the clean-up, repair and restoration.

"We have to sell the house," he told his wife.

"But we love this place!"

"I know, but we can't afford the leaks!"

Star Power

"I'm sorry," said the interviewer, closing the empty manila folder on her desk. "Apparently, I didn't get your resume."

"I didn't send one."

"You didn't?"

"No, I just made a call."

She looked puzzled.

"Well, let's go ahead," she said, picking up her pen.

"Great. What would you like to know?"

"Why don't you tell me a little about yourself?"

He chuckled.

"Don't you know who I am?"

She studied his face.

"I'm Phineas J. Whoopee."

She blushed.

"Oh, Senator Whoopee! I'm sorry. I guess I've only ever seen you on TV."

"No worries. It happens all the time."

"Well, your record in the Senate speaks for itself. Why don't you tell me what you did before you were a Senator?"

"I played golf."

"Golf?"

"Miniature golf actually."

"Miniature golf?"

"Yes. I won the Harris Cup."

"The Harris Cup?"

"I was the international miniature golf champion."

"Congratulations."

"Thank you."

"And your experience before that?"

"I was in the restaurant business."

"Interesting. Did you own restaurants?"

"No, I was an assistant manager."

"I see. And what were your responsibilities?"

"I mainly worked the drive-thru."

She cleared her throat.

"So you were elected to the Senate based on your fame as a miniature golfer?"

"It certainly helped."

She put down her pen.

"Senator, I'm sorry to be so direct, but can you tell me why you believe you're qualified to be the CEO of this company?"

"Star power."

"Pardon me?"

"People know me."

"And you think that's sufficient?"

"Well, it's worked pretty well for me so far."

"That it has."

He smiled.

"I think those are all my questions for now, sir. Do you have any questions for me?"

"Just one."

"Yes?"

"Is there a corporate jet?"

Trained

"Good morning, Charlotte," said the woman behind the desk. "And how is Bella today?"

"Good morning," said Charlotte, struggling to restrain the terrier pulling hard and barking excitedly at the end of her leash. "Bella's a little high-strung today."

"I can see that," said the woman, getting up and coming around the desk. "Well, maybe we'll give her some extra time outside this afternoon."

"Good idea," said Charlotte, looking frazzled.

But just as she was handing over the leash, Bella lunged into the air and broke free.

The two women ran after her, as Bella knew they would.

Eat Local

She hurried over to his table, flipping the page on her order pad with her thumb.

"Hi there," she said.

"Hello."

"Need a minute?"

"Any recommendations?"

"The beef on weck."

"Pardon me?"

"The beef on weck."

"Whack?"

"Weck."

"What?"

"*Weck*," she said, sounding irritated. "Roast beef on a kummel*weck* roll."

"A kummelweck roll?"

"Thin roll with salt and caraway seeds."

"With roast beef?"

"Yeah. Rare. Cut thin and topped with horseradish."

"I've never heard of it."

"It's a local favorite," she said, tapping her pen and rolling her eyes. "Yer in Buffalo."

"Okay," he said, feeling chastened. "I'll try it."

Lonely Body

"What should we do with the body?"

"Ditch it," he said. "It's of no use to us."

"Easier said than done."

"What do you mean?"

"I'd have to throw it in the dumpster."

"So?"

"Lenny, the dumpster's right outside. People would see."

"Wait until it gets dark then."

"That's no better."

"Why?"

"There's always a cop around."

Lenny sighed.

"You know, Brooks, you're my assistant. You're supposed to do what I say."

"Don't I always?" said Brooks, a scrawny, mousy-looking man.

"Not right now."

Brooks said nothing.

"I could fire you, you know," Lenny said.

"Go ahead," Brooks said with rare bravado.

"Maybe I will."

Lenny was sitting at his desk, a hunched mound of flesh with thin, gray hair combed over a head the size of a soccer ball.

"You'd have a hard time finding anybody who can do eyes like me," Brooks said.

"There are others."

"But nobody who can do them like me. Lips too."

"You're kind of full of yourself today, aren't you?"

"Just stating the facts."

Brooks seldom stood up to Lenny, but he knew the big man needed him, so he decided to push it.

"I won't even mention hair," he said.

"All right!" Lenny bellowed, slapping the desktop with his meaty palms. "I'll do it myself!"

He got up and waddled across the room, passing head after head, arranged in neat rows on narrow, wooden tables. Dozens of heads, each one anchored to a tabletop with a metal collar. Each was expressionless, staring blankly ahead. Some had hair. Others were bald. Some sported eyelashes and wore lipstick. Others were unadorned. Most were the heads of men and women. One row, though, was made up of the heads of children.

Finally, Lenny reached the body, propped up in the corner, wedged between rows of boxes stacked high against the walls. He wrapped his fleshy left arm around the naked torso and pulled it close. He grabbed hold of the head with his thick right hand and twisted it until it popped off with the sound of a bottle being uncorked.

He dropped the head on a table and dragged the decapitated body toward the door of the shop, his shop, where he had worked for nearly five decades, preparing plastic and fiberglass heads for storefronts all over the world.

Why, he wondered, during all that time, had only one arrived with a body?

About the Author

After a long career in the corporate world, Don Tassone has returned to his creative writing roots.

Musings is his ninth book. The others are the novels *Francesca* and *Drive* and the short story collections *Collected Stories, Snapshots, New Twists, Sampler, Small Bites* and *Get Back.* His novella, *The Liberation of Jacob Novak,* will be published in 2024.

Don and his wife Liz live in Loveland, Ohio. They have four children and nine grandchildren.

Visit Don at dontassone.com.

CPSIA information can be obtained
at www.ICGtesting.com
Printed in the USA
JSHW050922050323
38375JS00006BA/201